3 1432 00103 5920

D0502826

E
CHRIST-   Kasparavicius, Kestutis
MAS   Bear family's world tour Christmas

DISCARD

Boulder City Library
701 Adams Boulevard
Boulder City, NV 89005

The Bear Family's
World Tour Christmas

by

Kestutis Kasparavičius

DISCARD

Boulder City Library
701 Adams Boulevard
Boulder City, NV 89005
NOV 2003

H A R R Y   N .   A B R A M S ,   I N C . ,   P U B L I S H E R S

One cold November morning, Momma and Pappa Bear, and their children, Buddy, Theo, Jo-Jo, and Cher were preparing for the long winter ahead.

"Where shall we spend Christmas this year?" asked Father Bear.

"Let's go to Sri Lanka," said Buddy. "And visit our friends the Sun Bears."

"No," said Jo-Jo. "Let's go to Australia and see the Koala family."

"We must see Uncle and Auntie Teddy and our Teddy cousins like we do every year," said a worried little Cher.

"Why not have a world tour Christmas?" said Momma.

"And visit all our friends and family!" said Aunt Mona and Uncle Buster.

Everyone agreed that this was a wonderful plan. They set to work preparing their balloon house for the big trip.

Soon after, on a cold, clear night, they
all set off on their adventure. Momma
and Pappa Bear always liked to travel at
night because there was less traffic. The
spirit of the holidays filled the air.

In the morning, they arrived at the home of their good friends Mr. and Mrs. White in the far north. All the little ones were busy ice-fishing and playing house.

"Let's surprise them," whispered Cousin Rudy to Jo-Jo as they climbed down the ladder.

Mrs. White *was* surprised. "Look what Santa brought!" she exclaimed. "Now you can help me make Christmas cookies."

"Can I help *eat* the Christmas cookies?" asked Cousin Rudy, laughing.

"Where are we going next, Pappa?" asked Jo-Jo, back in their traveling house.

"We're off to sunny Peru," said Father as he steered. "Our friends the Spectacled Bears have lived there for years."

Peru was beautiful, and so different from home at Christmas time. It was hot and sunny. No one needed a winter coat. The Spectacled Bears had many presents waiting for their friends.

Next the family set off for Australia.

"The Koalas love Christmas!" said Aunt Mona.

When the Bears arrived with a gift of a Christmas tree they had picked up along the way, they discovered that their friends were already in the holiday spirit. They were decorating everything for the holiday— even the emus!

The family then set their traveling caps for Sri Lanka to visit the Sun Bears.

"Pappa, can Santa bring us an elephant?" asked little Cher.

"I suppose he could," Pappa answered, "if you will clean up after it."

Cher thought that over. "Maybe a kitten would be better," she said.

Soon the family was off to China. When they arrived they found that the Panda family was already greeting another visitor—Grandpa Panda, who paddled up in his boat full of gifts. An extra present floated along behind!

After all the traveling and visiting, the family finally arrived at their favorite aunt and uncle's house. Uncle and Auntie Teddy and the cousins were so happy to see them! This year, like every year, they exchanged presents right away. Uncle Teddy had always wanted to become a balloon pilot himself. He was delighted when Pappa gave him an honorary flight medal as a gift.

"This will look great with my winter coat!" said Uncle Teddy.

Inside the house, all the children worked together to set up holiday decorations in the playroom. There was even a toy Santa with a gold star!

"I wish Santa would hurry up and come," said little Cher. "When will they call us into the great room?"

Then the children heard their Auntie Teddy. "Children, come and meet our special guest!"

Santa Bear! He had a huge bag of presents, and he winked at the children when they entered the room.

"Oh, my!" cried the children, as they did each year.

The children gave Santa milk and cookies, and then they took him to a globe on the dresser.

"Let us show you where we have been," cried the children. Buddy used a pointer to show each stop the family had made, and the children put on the clothes and hats that they had been given on their trip.

"Like me, you have visited so many places this time of year," said Santa. "What a perfect holiday!"

"A perfect *Christmas* holiday!" chimed little Cher.

Based on a story by Paul Maar

Designer: Becky Terhune

Library of Congress Cataloging-in-Publication Data

Kasparavičius, Kestutis.
The bear family's world tour Christmas / by Kestutis Kasparavičius.
    p. cm.
Summary: Momma and Pappa Bear and their four children have a world tour
Christmas, visiting friends and family in China, Australia, and other
countries, and sharing special holiday traditions in each place.
  ISBN 0-8109-0573-6
  [1. Bears—Fiction. 2. Christmas—Fiction. 3. Voyages and
travels—Fiction.] I. Title.
  PZ7.K15428 Be 2002
  [E]—dc21
                                                              2001056740

Copyright © 1997 by Esslinger Verlag J.F. Schreiber GmbH, Esslingen – Wien
Text copyright © 2002 Harry N. Abrams, Inc.

Published in 2002 by Harry N. Abrams, Incorporated, New York
All rights reserved. No part of the contents of this book may be
reproduced without the written permission of the publisher.

Printed and bound in Belgium
10 9 8 7 6 5 4 3 2 1

▲

Harry N. Abrams, Inc.
100 Fifth Avenue
New York, N.Y. 10011
www.abramsbooks.com

Abrams is a subsidiary of
LA MARTINIÈRE
G R O U P E